One day Bear who lived in the forest and Eagle who lived in the mountains began to shout. Great angry waves of meaningless noise rolled round Moose's head.

MICHAEL FOREMAN
MOOSE

This paperback edition first published in 2014 by Andersen Press Ltd., 20 Vauxhall Bridge Road, London SW1V 2SA.
First published in Great Britain in 1971 by Hamish Hamilton Children's Books. Text copyright © Michael Foreman, 1971.
The rights of Michael Foreman to be identified as the author and illustrator of this work have been asserted by
him in accordance with the Copyright, Designs and Patents Act, 1988. All rights reserved.
Printed and bound in Singapore by Tien Wah Press. British Library Cataloguing in Publication Data available. ISBN 978 1 78344 101 3
10 9 8 7 6 5 4 3 2 1

Moose was just an ordinary moose. He worked a little too hard, got cross in hot weather and was poor. What he liked best was to sit outside in the cool of the evening and sing quietly to himself.

Bear and Eagle shouted all day. Moose couldn't stand it. He went to see Bear.

"Excuse me, Bear, but why do you shout at me?"

"SHOUT at YOU?" shouted Bear. "I didn't know you EXISTED. WHO ARE YOU?"

"Moose," said Moose.

"HA HA! Very amoosing," roared Bear. "I am not shouting at YOU. I'm shouting at that CRAZY BALD EAGLE!"

Moose went to see Eagle. "Excuse me, Eagle," said Moose, "but are you shouting at me or at Bear?"

"I AM SHOUTING AT THAT FLEA-BITTEN BEAR!" bellowed Eagle. "And I'll shout at you if you don't vamoose, Moose."

By the time Moose arrived home, the shouting was louder than ever. Poor Moose was in despair. "Oh well," he said, "sticks and stones may break my bones but words will never hurt me."

But the very next morning the sticks and stones began.
Bear threw sticks at Eagle and Eagle threw stones at
Bear. Some of the sticks and stones fell short and crashed
around Moose's house.

Moose was very frightened. He began using the sticks and stones to build a shelter. He built and built, dodging everything Bear and Eagle threw.

Eagle ordered his friends to help throw stones.

Bear made the other animals throw sticks.

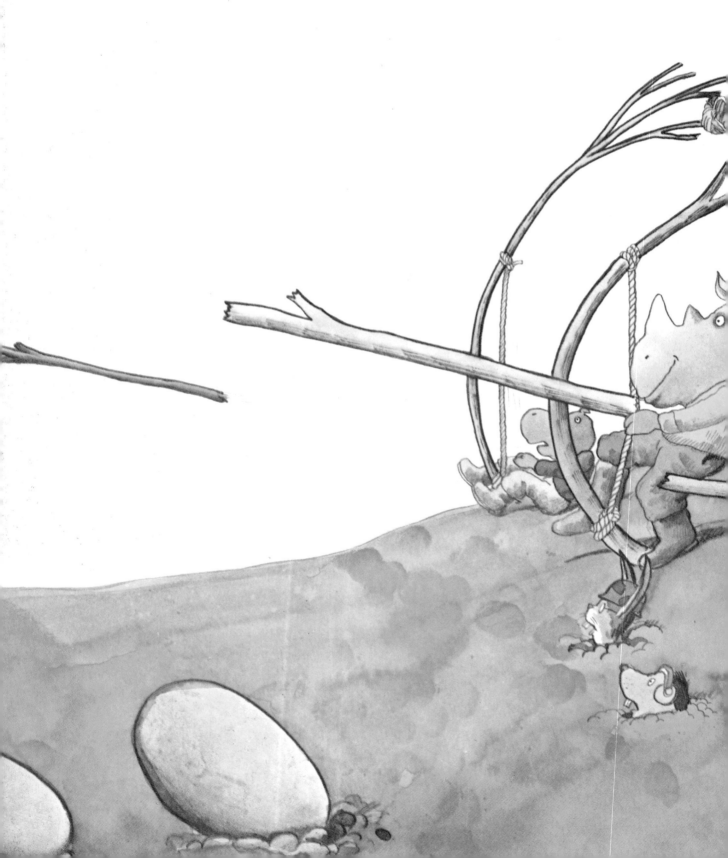

Moose worked all through the day and all through the night. He became so interested in his shelter that he forgot about Bear and Eagle and took no more notice of the shouting. His building grew larger and more splendid, and all the animals except Bear and Eagle laid down their sticks and stones and came to watch the building grow.

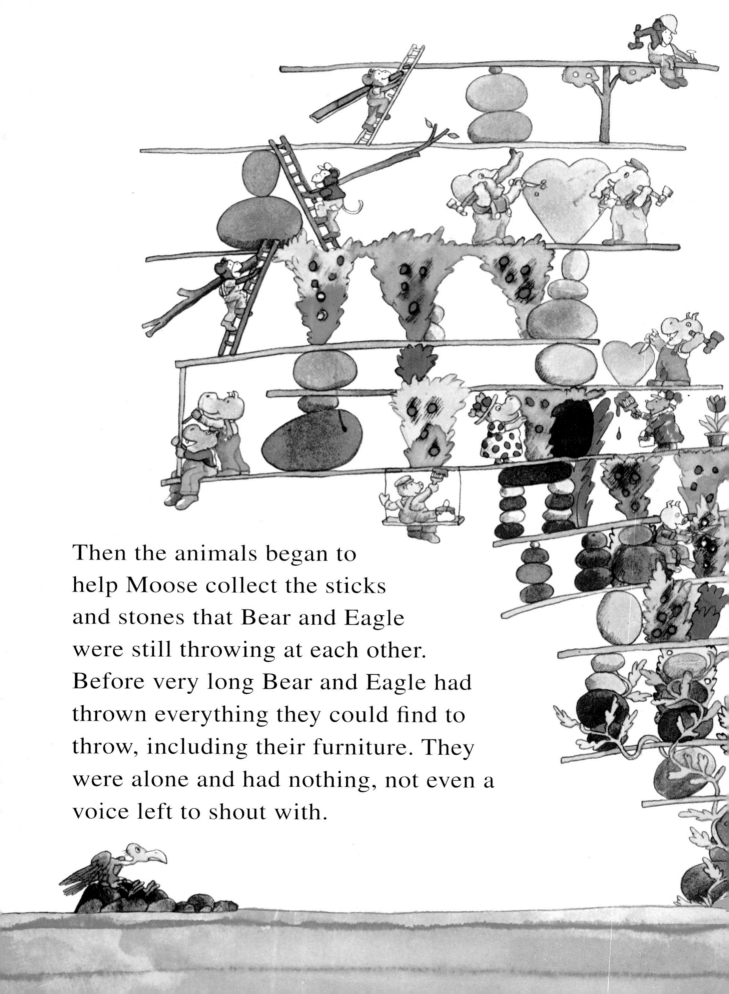

Then the animals began to
help Moose collect the sticks
and stones that Bear and Eagle
were still throwing at each other.
Before very long Bear and Eagle had
thrown everything they could find to
throw, including their furniture. They
were alone and had nothing, not even a
voice left to shout with.

Every morning after that the animals arrived with ideas for improving the building. They added a Mooseum, an Amoosement Park and even a Moosic Hall.

And in the evenings they sang songs by the light of the moon.

And then they went home, still singing.

Moose was content. He sang to the stars and sometimes, far off in the distance, he heard Bear and Eagle rumbling away to themselves. "Shouting and fighting didn't do them any good," said Moose. "Perhaps one day they will discover that it is much more fun to sing."